I0538877

Jeffrey Andrew was diagnosed with schizoaffective disorder. Due to this, he was admitted to three mental hospitals. Over the course of time, he experienced delusions and hallucinations either on television or people walking around him. Jeffrey believes he is prescribed the correct medication, but he will never know if the delusions and hallucinations are real or false. Will they ever go away? All he can do is live the rest of his life with this disorder.

This book is dedicated to the people in my life. Thank you for believing in me. I have had many "ups and downs" as time went by. I believe the obstacles make me fight harder in this thing we call "life."

I did it. I wrote a book.

Jeffrey Andrew

SEEING AND HEARING IMAGINARY THINGS

SCHIZOAFFECTIVE DISORDER

AUSTIN MACAULEY PUBLISHERS™

LONDON · CAMBRIDGE · NEW YORK · SHARJAH

Copyright © Jeffrey Andrew (2020)

All rights reserved. No part of this publication may be reproduced, distributed, or transmitted in any form or by any means, including photocopying, recording, or other electronic or mechanical methods, without the prior written permission of the publisher, except in the case of brief quotations embodied in critical reviews and certain other noncommercial uses permitted by copyright law. For permission requests, write to the publisher.

Any person who commits any unauthorized act in relation to this publication may be liable to criminal prosecution and civil claims for damages.

Ordering Information:
Quantity sales: special discounts are available on quantity purchases by corporations, associations, and others. For details, contact the publisher at the address below.

Publisher's Cataloging-in-Publication data
Andrew, Jeffrey
Seeing and Hearing Imaginary Things: Schizoaffective Disorder

ISBN 9781641827461 (Paperback)
ISBN 9781641827478 (Hardback)
ISBN 9781645364696 (ePub e-book)

Library of Congress Control Number: 2019915028

www.austinmacauley.com/us

First Published (2020)
Austin Macauley Publishers LLC
40 Wall Street, 28th Floor
New York, NY 10005
USA

mail-usa@austinmacauley.com
+1 (646) 512-5767

Austin Macauley Publishers believed in my manuscript. I would like to acknowledge the time and effort the publishing company has put forth.

I appreciate the professionalism the company exemplified.

A Hidden Agenda

A creepy house stands in darkness during daylight shadows. In a dirty entrance, a wall hangs symbolism. Crosses hang everywhere. They are hanging to make Jeffrey believe in Jesus Christ's past, claiming he is "The Son of God."

Jeffrey attended church in his younger years. While very involved, he never read the Bible. Understanding the translation made it hard for him to comprehend "The Scriptures."

People approach Jeffrey to force his beliefs or make a decision in life before he passes. In the past, mishaps occurred on Christmas. Till today, Jeffrey recognizes the personal family problems that arose.

"Why should Jeffrey believe in Jesus Christ? Christmas was horrible numerous times!"

Jesus was a major part of the congregation because of the cross in front of us. Jeffrey used to goof around with his young friends during church services. During sermons, sleep overcame him every now and then.

Jeffrey believes church is great for children. They are surrounded by people that mean well. Some of those children grow up and have misfortunes and social disasters. For Jeffrey, his faith began to waiver in 2017 when admitted to a mental hospital as an outpatient.

Jeffrey gathers his thoughts.

He knocks on the solid wooden door. Small and rowdy dogs bark as Jeffrey and Rose ring the doorbell. No answer.

Later, Jeffrey finds out there are children that don't answer the door to strangers. He knew this but was eager to find out what the rental house looked like inside.

Jeffrey returns to the house, and the tenant lets him in the establishment. Creeping in the home without the required property manager. The family is there.

Two children are in their bedrooms, relaxing, as Jeffrey walks around the corners of the house. The tenant leasing the house said his wife was helping him pack for their departure.

The gentleman sounded feminine. Was he lying to Jeffrey about having a wife? Was he really married or were the children kidnapped?

Was danger coming his way?

A Living Drum Set

Practicing his trap set, which is dark green and beautiful. Drums sitting there full of experience and banging. Drumheads are dead and ready for replacement.

He hears a squeak and jumps off the drum throne. Looking at the cymbal stand arm. It bends and forms a human metal arm like the movie *Terminator 2*. Melting and shaping take over as the metal holding his drum set moves his drums in the air.

This looks like a challenge to him.

He jumps on the drum seat, and the chair unexpectedly moves around. Riding a mechanical bull crosses his mind.

Hoofs form around the base of the back legs of the drum throne. Then, hoofs begin to dig into the ground in front of the bass drum.

Jeffrey reaches hard for the drums and cymbals, and it is second nature. He can play blindfolded. The drum set becomes part of his inner brainpower.

Sweat drips from the green rack tom because it resonates so hard. Slam after slam causes those vibrations to almost cause a circular waterfall. The maple drum warps a little and then distorts back to shape.

The 16-inch floor tom is perfectly deep. Jeffrey's eyeglasses tremble on his nose, creating a temporary red mark. Five stroke, 7 stroke roll combinations with the 14-inch snare drum and 16-inch. It sounds like thunder and actual lightning striking a tree!

All he has to do is think of a drumbeat, and the drums move for him. Cymbals too.

Has Jeffrey conquered his drum set?

Angling Shoes

Gliding through the grass with multitudes of thorns in the land of green and beige. Fishing shoes and socks are covered in prickles.

Schizophrenia makes Jeffrey count the continuous bristles while sitting on the bed. One after the other. Pebbles are next. Digging through cracks and traction of the shoes. Fingernails and tips burrowing one side to the other.

It is worth it. Big-mouthed bass were caught in fighting motion. Knees bending back and forth. Thighs flexing and leg muscles popping out. What a blast it is!

Grabbing the rod and reel in beginning mode. The right hand wraps around the bottom of the rod, and the reel goes in between the middle and fourth finger. After that, the index finger pulls on the fishing line and locks on the rod to secure the hold. The bail is released, and the bait is ready to be tossed.

Looking around for a place to land his lure after casting. Bubbles surface through the water to the top. Little fins barely present themselves as fish swim around.

The angler walks a little to the left to avoid hooking algae. Poppers become his focused taste of bait. You tug 1, 3, 2, 5, or any number of times while retrieving your popper.

This type of fishing is fun for Jeffrey. Finally, after a few times casting, a big-mouthed bass attacks his popper. The bass grabs the lure bait and flows in the air.

Pulling and reeling till the barely slimy lip is squeezed with a thumb and index finger. So heavy. One bass is dropped on the ground accidentally.

Tennis shoes are swapped with sandals.

Do shoes make a difference when fishing?

Baby Shower

The blockade marked orange and white stands in front of Jeffrey while sitting in his SUV. He looks around and sees two bodies of water. There are two posts with signs on them. Jeffrey takes a gander at both. Individually at a time. Both posts have a "No trespassing" policy on the signs.

Before Jeffrey drops off Rose at a baby shower, Rose tells Jeffrey that people fish out there all the time. He gathers his fishing equipment from his vehicle. Makes his way to the large waterbody. Puts down the backpack cooler and starts to fish.

Jeffrey does not carry anything else with him. He decides to fish with one lure. If he loses it, Jeffrey will go back to his SUV to grab another lure. He has quite a selection of crank bait. It seems to be doing very well.

Jeffrey is concerned about Rose. She is experiencing serious hallucinations and delusions. She is starting to question her disability diagnosis. She thinks she has Schizoaffective Disorder like Mr. Jeffrey Andrew. Hopefully, her friends understand her condition. Jeffrey carries his phone in his back pocket to accept her potential phone call.

A couple fishing casts go by. Jeffrey sees a police officer pass on his right side. Jeffrey's fishing license is expired, so he goes to the store to get a new one. Jeffrey must remind Rose to bring her driver's license to get a new fishing license. She never carries her driver's license with her.

They fish together all the time. He does not want Rose to get a fishing violation ticket. She will probably get embarrassed, and Jeffrey would blame it on himself.

Jeffrey tries fishing at a location which he and Rose scoped out earlier. A child catches a fish, but Jeffrey has no bites at all. His lure would get close from the retrieval and little minnows would chase Jeffrey's bait. That is the only action he receives in that area.

Jeffrey's cellphone rings, and it is Rose. She is ready to be picked up from the baby shower. Rose made a gift that she called a "Stormpooper." The motorcycle was made of diapers. The Stormpooper on top of the diaper motorcycle was a stuffed animal with a Stormtrooper Halloween mask. Jeffrey never expected to see such an adorable gift for the soon-to-be baby.

Jeffrey loads his vehicle with his fishing supplies to pick up Rose. She packs him two chocolate chip cookies in between two plastic plates. Upon his arrival, Jeffrey eats them right away because he loves cookies.

Rose seems like she does not have a hard time with delusions and hallucinations. At night, Jeffrey asks her how her mental disorder was during the day. Rose says she saw a man hanging from a noose. Banging against the door.

Will doctors ever give a proper diagnosis?

16

Baseball Nephews

Jeffrey walks along the silver metal fence. Not knowing what to expect. He looks to his right and sees baseball players wearing hoodies. He has never seen that look on baseball players. They are young yet throwing the ball hard. The team walks in a single-file line to the dugout. The other team remains on the field because they are the "Home Team."

Jeffrey rushes around home plate and sees his sister. She waves him down to get his attention. As he dashes over there, his brother-in-law is entering the baseball players on his computer.

Jeffrey's brother-in-law loves to do baseball statistics for his son. He can tell his sister's husband loves to be around his child. He participates as much as he can while one of Jeffrey's nephews is growing up.

They have tried to get Jeffrey's nephew to workout. Last time Jeffrey went to their house, a weight bench lay on the ground. A light shined on the bench to give it a glorifying presence. Weights were on the ground to do curls. A bar had weight plates on it to do bench press. Jeffrey was very impressed. He believes this baseball nephew is ready to get even more serious.

Jeffrey started watching his nephew since he was a youngster. He still considers him a young kid. He is growing up faster than he thought. Jeffrey always knew he would be tall one day. He has analyzed his height from far away but not up close. He is the same height or taller.

Jeffrey's other nephew is younger. He is talented and plays baseball, too. It is hard to view this nephew's baseball games because he lives far away. Jeffrey misses this nephew and cannot wait to see him play again.

Will these nephews play baseball against each other in the future?

Bell Trees

Bell trees falling like
Doves from above
They swing and swing
To find some love
Fighting and fighting…it
Doesn't work…they
Look at each other and
Feel the rough…their
Mind is so quick but
Kinda slow…they
Emerse each other's
Body love…they
Get their last peck
While they fall
The man bird realizes
The distance is small
The man bird looks again
Realizes the water…is
Deep and spins
He tells his girlfriend…we're
Safe…again.

Bird

He looks forward into a dream. He takes a step into the wet drops of water that relieve his feet.

He turns the water warmer then colder to find the right temperature to fight the burning in his feet. Toes separate then come together in undeniable pain. Is it up or down?

Feet start to trample around splashing rapids into the river that's beneath him. A boulder rises to lift him to safety. Tons of beautiful fish swim around him.

The fish swim faster and faster to fill their gills with air. Jumping out of the water, they look content as the temperature rises.

The water gets hotter and the fish start to bounce off his feet because they feel like they are going to pass.

Bouncing all over the boulder, he tells them, "Hey little ones. It'll be okay."

Still. The different colored fish bounce higher as to reach the wind blowing around them. It starts to rain.

Drip. Drop. Drip. Drop.

He looks down and the fish skirmish, twirl, fling, and get lucky to feel their first drop. The water spatters into his eye and sees a reflection off the scales of the fish. It's the sun.

Glaring as if mirror images sparkle in different directions. It is hard to look at a single fish scale because they are intriguing and remarkable. Exemplifying a painting shaped like a fish.

A bird enters the mirrored painting from right to left. What kind of bird is it?

Blue Ground

On the blue ground
There is sound
Nice cool fungus
All around
Jump up
And down
I want to mug down
Like hopping on the moon
It is around noon
It is time for my dinner break
I think I'll have a steak
Hop on over to the grill
My thoughts are not still
Stack up the charcoal
The charcoal is in a hole
Go ahead and get it wet
Weather's hot and start to sweat
Light the coal safely
I don't want to waste any
My friend falls asleep
By myself and cook to keep
In my head is a song
Hopefully it is strong.

Celebrities

The color red. It is all rolled up. The layer waiting for the next ultimate experience, for those who have been there and who have not. People unroll the red mass to form "The Red Carpet."

Celebrities get together before an awards ceremony. Celebs work hard on their entertainment industry projects. Recognition and progress is achieved in superstar lives when they win the prestigious awards. The icons that do not win are still considered household, overachiever names.

These stars transform their personalities to become someone else in a story. Voiceovers are very creditable too. Watching them on a computer, television, or movie screen is believable. The way these personalities speak in a certain tone and dress make performances interesting.

Jeffrey always wanted to sit in the VIP section and view the celebrities in the expensive outfits. Sometimes, brands pay a celeb to wear an outfit or jewelry. The women look stunning in the colorful dresses. Necklaces, earrings, bracelets, and rings are very expensive and striking.

After the interviews, celebrities are called into the theater for the award show. The seats in the front have nominee names and pictures.

The superstars receive expensive "Goodie Bags." They also eat and drink after the show. This is a life Jeffrey always dreamed of.

Will Jeffrey accomplish his life-long dreams or is Schizophrenia believing the unbelievable?

Climbing to the Cry

When I cry
I start to weep
I sit down
Beneath my feet
Please God
I climb so high
Another birdie in the sky
Oh my God. I hate to lie
In the sky
Legs start to fry
I'm so high
I start to sigh
Oh my God. I'm gonna cry.

Colorado House

They stop at a marijuana dispensary on the way to the Colorado house. Jeffrey steps out of the car door on to snow that covers the parking lot. He takes the staircase to the right as he marches his way up to a different legal realm.

An employee looks at Jeffrey's driver's license to make sure he is old enough. He stamps Jeffrey's hand. It is time to visit the next room. The room that has all different types of "weed." Jeffrey looks around and cannot believe his eyes.

The salespeople run around the store to produce a high profit for the day. Jumping on countertops to write on chalkboards. Here, they mention special deals. Jeffrey cannot believe the excitement and energy in the dispensary.

Jeffrey walks out of the door toward the staircase. Some Coloradans, or Coloradicals, pass him with high energy. They know it is time to hook up with "pot." Jeffrey approaches the vehicle and jumps in the back seat. He is prepared for the Colorado house.

The driver, passenger, and Jeffrey drive through the Rocky Mountains. It is a beautiful sight. Ice caps and snow is everywhere! Luckily, Jeffrey is wearing hiking boots and clothes to keep him warm.

A snowplow is called in before they arrive at the house. Tire marks are engraved in the snow. The rental car makes it up the mountain about 9,000 feet above sea level. Jeffrey chews gum to "pop" his ears.

Jeffrey puts his legal marijuana in his suitcase. He grabs his luggage first. There is a security pad to open the garage door to the house. The passenger types in the security code, and the garage opens. Jeffrey walks up the steep stairs to the garage door of the house. He brings his suitcase to his room. Afterwards, he grabs everybody else's luggage from the trunk of the car and brings it to their room.

Jeffrey works his way downstairs with "pot" in hand. He does not want to make it obvious. The other two people want him to wait until the sun goes down. He lights a "joint" outside the house to experience the Colorado "smoke." He listens to *One* by the band "Metallica." Jeffrey cranks it up.

Jeffrey lights a cigarette and enjoys the mountainous view. He has gloves on and a warm hat on his head. Jeffrey is required to ash in a bottle with water in it. The bottle has a wide lip. This makes it convenient for Jeffrey. Jeffrey stands up after the song is over and gathers firewood.

There is a huge pile of firewood near the side of the house. Jeffrey grabs a piece of wood and places it on a wooden stump. He hacks at it with an axe. This forms quarter-sized pieces of firewood to put in the fire pit. Also, he chops pieces very small to make kindle wood.

The fire is built and ready to be lit aflame. Jeffrey puts lighter fluid on it and uses his lighter to ignite it. He sees different designs in the flames. It is like painting on a canvas in 3D. He pushes the sticks and logs around to see different artistic objects. For example, he sees a dune buggy and later a horse.

The fire grows in capacity.

Jeffrey wants to scream to hear his voice echo in the mountains. He cannot. The other two people are inside the house. They might get mad or worried about Jeffrey's safety. The neighbors might be concerned, too.

The fire breathes its last breath, and it is dinnertime. They call out to Jeffrey. He puts the screen lid on the fire pit. Jeffrey heads inside and enjoys a healthy dinner.

This is one experience Jeffrey partook in at the Colorado house.

What sober encounters will Jeffrey run into at the Colorado house?

Connection

Darkness kicks on the mood. Eyes move around every millimeter at a time. Blue and brown all over the place. Maybe blue and blue, brown and brown, and green combinations. Eyes fit a perfect correlation.

Faces get two inches far from each other. Feeling in the middle of the forehead starts to tickle. Her left eye looks in his right eye. Right eye looks in his left eye. The two get even closer.

Tips of the noses brush from left to right, continuously for fifteen seconds. She cannot help it. Her beautiful eyes close because of the emotional sensation. This is delivered to her nose, breasts, and heart.

Beautiful eyes open slowly without a blink. Jeffrey cannot believe what he sees when her colored, shiny eyes are halfway open. Glare comes out like an upside down half-moon.

Is it friendship, possible relationship, or love up close?

Can we read each other's connection through colored retinas or is it the eyelids that droop a little?

A moment like this is special because you earn a position closer to an individual.

In the past, you get a glimpse of the person; body, clothes, and hair. Sometimes charging an inner battery to run around body obstacles to get a peek at the point of interest.

Will I marry that someone?

Continuous Cartwheels

Three people are outside in the fertilized backyard. The grass is freshly cut and trimmed around the trees. It reminds Jeffrey of playing soccer on a Saturday morning. Lake water is beautiful as the breeze sweeps past their bodies.

The deck is organized with a little dust on wooden boundaries. Two grills sit on the deck waiting to be used; charcoal and a propane tank grill. Two people look at Jeffrey in the sunny, blue-skied weather wondering what he does for fun. There is so much activity a person can do in the paradise-stricken atmosphere.

Fishing rods rest outside in the corner with lake water on the fishing line. These rods and reels are used a lot toward the end of Jeffrey's stay at the lake house in Willis, Texas. Two friends buy a boat and take Jeffrey with them almost every day to cast fishing lines in incredible fishing coves.

Jeffrey always dreamed of fishing in coves like these. He spent most of his weekends as a child at the lake house and never made it out to these locations. His family had a waterski boat, which was long in length, deep, and heavy. A troll motor would have been nice to have bolted down, also.

Jeffrey tends to the two people that are in the backyard with him. It is a mother and child.

The daughter looks at him and says, "Do some cartwheels."

Jeffrey, the occupant of the lake house, looks down the grassy hill. Leading with his left hand, Jeffrey does one cartwheel after the other. Mentally, he cannot believe it. He's done handstand pushups against a wall but never executed gymnastics like this.

He looks down at the grass when his head is toward the ground. His head looks up after that, causing dizziness and lightheadedness. It doesn't matter. Jeffrey keeps going and going. His body looks like a Chinese throwing star rolling down the hill.

A glimpse of the rocks and lake is near and approaching. Motion of his cartwheels is broken.

Jeffrey falls on purpose by the edge of the rocks. Snakes are sometimes located within the cracks and on top of the rocks, sitting down on the soft grass. Shakiness fades as he looks at the existent border of the rocks and lake.

The mother and child watch him recuperate on the land. Jeffrey marches up to them. They look at him in disbelief.

What would happen if he doesn't fall?

Delivery

Jeffrey sits on the cushion attached to the new leather couch. A light wind from the fan and air conditioning passes by his ears. It passes Jeffrey's eardrums into his body.

He doesn't know what it is. A passion for a breath or a deliverance to a part that distinguishes some sort of life-form. Is it true? Jeffrey's organ passes an involuntary light to another organ.

The organ thinks, *Please relax and let me function.*
Jeffrey tries to build a sense of relief. Steaming warmth, cold restitute, and a significant change find his sensitive heart.

He bleeds and bleeds within his select, entrapped, skin-layered body form. Forced rivers and sewer lines spew red fizz and natural objects to Jeffrey's breath.

Will deliverance keep Jeffrey alive?

Discovered an Aquifer

Jumping into water in front of him. Scuba gear is attached to Jeffrey's body. Feet are entrapped in foot fins and a frameless scuba mask wraps around his head.

Holding his scuba mask, a little water sneaks in the side and wets Jeffrey's eyes slightly. No worries. Jeffrey holds the mask, exhales through his nose, and blows the excess water out.

Weights on Jeffrey's belt pull down the body to this cave-like structure which runs perpendicular to the earth's surface.

Venturing down the little waterway, the surface is very detailed. Luckily, a waterproof headlamp is in his possession. Jeffrey reaches another cave. Gravel and sandstones are present as he uses his light to scan the surface. Jeffrey keeps going further into the water cave.

Jeffrey's snorkel accidentally falls out of his mouth and water enters the throat slowly. He cannot believe it. Jeffrey makes it to the top of the cave and there is a space to breathe.

The water tastes delicious. Jeffrey takes another taste and cannot believe his taste buds. How far down is he located after he jumps in the water?

Rushing back to the starting point, Jeffrey takes off his foot fins, scuba tank, frameless mask, and belt. Then, he pulls down the top of the wet suit to dry and get a little tan.

Jeffrey runs to the first person and tells them about the minerals and rocks located in the cave. Jeffrey wonders if he would receive money for this discovery.

Jeffrey says, "We might be able to pump water out of a cave I discovered. You know. Build a water well. The water is very tasteful."

Is this the middle of Earth?

Dog Dreams

A web created on the ceiling is attached to a plastic coat. A neutral-colored spider didn't put it there but a person trying to survive.

Darkness covers the area while dressing for the next step; eating in the plastic container which was purchased in the store. The tent has many pockets to store items on a camping trip.

Dim light shines throughout the dome to give a sense of awareness and direction. What's to the left, center, right, and back?

A headlamp is placed in the web to create a ceiling light. Jeffrey puts the headlamp on its highest setting. Rose thinks it is a great idea for Jeffrey to use the lamp to light up the tent. Jeffrey can tell she is getting into the camping trip.

Jeffrey and Rose plan the trip last minute. All they need is fifteen dollars for the campsite. Rose makes four sandwiches for the journey and goes with Jeffrey to the store to buy affordable necessities. A big blue and white cooler is where food and extra drinks are stored. They buy ice when they arrive at the entrance of Huntsville National Park.

After an eventful day at the camping grounds, dinner is cooked along with dessert. Jeffrey, Rose, and the dog relax in the tent. Jeffrey and Rose kiss.

The muscular pupster named "Dragster" lays down taking small yet deep breaths. Relaxed on the comfortable ground, the short-haired dog is in a world of relaxation and deep dreams. Dragster rolls over and makes whining noises.

What do dogs visualize in their dreams?

Drifting Dream

The astronaut stares at the human being across the green floor to see what he is thinking. He can see a slight whirlwind leak out of the ears of the defender.

Looking through the guided light, a sense of passion discovers his likings.

The audience cheers as he stands in the uniform spacesuit with his favorite number on it. Spectators are locked into chairs, so they do not drift through the air. Audience's spacesuit battery charge is safe after strapped in. Bottom of the cup holder charges spacesuits.

Batter speaks through his face-guard attachment. Third base coach orders a homerun attempt. Buttons on spacesuit light up a blue color as the code is punched in. Lights flicker and flash so code cannot be read by the defense.

A bat shoots out of the spacesuit. The arms lower and phalanges grip the bat tightly yet comfortably. Forearms bounce back and forth, finding a mechanical balance to move through zero gravity.

The protector of the ball looks the catcher square in the eyes. Shakes his head slowly to fight the gravity-less atmosphere. Strains his arm to reach the catcher's desired glove-colored light.

The light glimmers one spark at a time.

How long will it take the batter to run around the bases if he hits the ball?

Egg Rocket

The blue lounge chair is cocked back to resemble an astronaut taking off with little jet ignitors underneath it. The egg-shaped rocket has the most beautiful and strongest fishing pole strapped down on his left side.

A fellow makes a lure with a moon, neon-colored skirt. This is his favorite lure of all time. The lure is pinned to the top of the transparent rocket egg to see it when he is thinking of his daughter back home on Earth.

The male loves the transparent egg that Jeffrey has built for him. While floating in space toward the moon, everything is clear. There is no color except for the Earth, sun, and moon.

All of a sudden, his spacecraft starts to shake! He doesn't see it. It is a black hole that shoots toward the moon.

He has a fancy spacewatch on that is consistent and linked with Jeffrey's launchpad. It blinks rapidly as if it is running out of a battery charge. The battery is built by Jeffrey, so it cannot be low in charge.

The egg rocket speeds up but quits shaking. The man on the spacecraft can see a dark crater approaching. He grabs the lure, which is attached to the top of the egg rocket and kisses it. Thoughts of his daughter rush through his head.

The gentleman slams his left hand on the fishing pole. He whips the moon, neon-colored lure toward the fishing line. He slides the line through the line attachment on the lure and ties his strongest knot.

The moon gets closer, nearer, and within landing distance. The man hits a button, which is located to his lower right. This is supposed to turn on the ignitors of the egg-shaped rocket.

Jeffrey and the man in the spacecraft fill it with Supreme gas at a gas station before liftoff, at 3:00 AM when civilians are asleep.

Transporting the egg rocket is easy. All they have to do is load it in a truck and tie it down proportionately. The curvature structure is perfect and can bend if necessary.

The man feels the moon's presence. Both ignitors come out and are ready for landing.

The rocket starts to flip, unexpectedly, as it nears a location on the moon. The ignitors spray gasoline into zero gravity but don't stop the flipping and turning. All he can do is wait.

The spacecraft crashes on to the moon's surface. The male does not feel the bang because it is well built. It spins and bends until stopping at a nonintentional location.

Communications with the launchpad do not exist, so he decides to make it worth his while. The fishing rod is ready for his ultimate fishing experience. The noble man grabs it with excitement.

Spacewalking is easy for him. The fella lifts weights and does cardio workouts at the gym on a regular basis. As much as the guy works out, sweat pours from his forehead.

His body feels like he took a bath while lying in the egg rocket.

Sweat begins to fade like air drying without a towel at a pool or at the beach. The fishing rod and reel is in his left hand. He cannot believe it. A body of water is in his vision. He strives for the water, one foot after the other.

Long leaps are what it takes. Summersault, back, and twisted flips are fun for him. Finally, he reaches his destiny to fish on the moon. Cool shoes are mounted into the ground as he slides six feet on the moon's surface.

Different bright, moon-colored fish fly above the water doing acrobatic flips and turns. He cannot believe his eyes. This is a dream come true.

The man does not want to waste any time. Looking all around, the biggest fish flies his way while fighting zero gravity. He casts his beautiful lure in space. Casts are so good. Hitting targets is easy for the man no matter what the conditions.

Lure goes up, down, to the side, and back around. The man knows exactly how to travel the lure bait. A neon-colored moon fish goes for it. The fish does loops and circles in the atmosphere. It is the retrieval of his life.

Spacewatch makes a noise. It is Jeffrey.

He asks the man on the moon, "Are you okay, my friend?"

The moon angler says, "I caught me one."

The gentleman has power as a fishing god to do whatever he wants on the planet Earth and moon.

Who knows what he can do on the sun?

Eternal Love

I stare into her eyes and
This is what I see
A reflection of my smile that
Makes her express glee
We hold hands and swing our arms till
We feel a breeze
Dance around and feel the sun and
Almost start to sneeze
We've been together for a while and
It has been complete
We like to see each other and
Decide to stay up late
Holding hard for so long
I write a love song
Deep down within their hearts
Love will never be gone.

Extreme Love

When I'm alone
I take a seat
Deep down inside
I feel a beat
My mind drifts
Really hard
Musicality is a reward
Is there a girl
For this man
One that will follow and
Hold his hand
Look at me every day
Down and up
Will she have
A little pup
She's been through a lot and
So have I
Sometimes she stops and
Starts to cry
I am there for her
With no doubt
We lean toward
A different route

Press our faces
Cheek to cheek
Extreme love is what I seek.

Failure Is Success

Growing up, Jeffrey was taught to swim and how to dry off with a towel after swimming. It sounds stereotypical, and it is.

His parents forced thought in his head. This is the correct way to do everything. But the towel dries everyone differently.

As Jeffrey moves further along in life, he learns and perceives percussion in a different light.

Jeffrey's successes are not monetary. They are achievements such as medals, which he adds to his collection of swim team ribbons, soccer trophies/patches, Cub Scout Merit badges, Indian Guides, and various other achievements.

When Jeffrey's high school rock band formed, he thought of the new friends and relationships he would make. Also, wondering what the musical instruments would sound like when meshed together. The members that played and sang with Jeffrey had their differences. They plucked, exhaled, and listened like a towel touching your shoulder.

Growing up, Jeffrey's band watched bands on television. They saw what they thought were their successes. Playing in front of many people is considered a success to the rock band.

They put together that band in their freshman summer in college. Practice after practice, the band formed an alliance. Their friends from high school did their routines during the day that summer. The band felt like they didn't see anyone. They didn't force the music for any purpose. The college rock band enjoyed each other's company.

At the end of summer break, they had ONE gig. The band told their friends about the show, all kinds of friends.

The venue was dark. Jeffrey had never been in a place that had microphones, stands, and speakers. It was very mysterious because he was used to bright places.

The rock band's equipment was set up, and they waited to perform. Jeffrey did not think any of their friends were gonna show up.

Did venues let in young people?

The friends that showed up said they missed the musical group all summer. People from their high school that they didn't know showed up too.

Jeffrey kind of felt like a failure because they didn't make much money after practicing all summer long. But they succeeded in combining the different musical applications, which had granted them.

Jeffrey has tried all different types of things in life that brought no monetary value. Non-profit organizations, camp counseling, and things he thought helped people. Sometimes, people were enlightened. Sometimes, Jeffrey wasn't sure.

Jeffrey believes success is making a difference in yourself and others. It might feel like a failure, but that's okay.

What are good things in life? There are materials all around us. Jeffrey is still looking for the right answer.

Do people ever find the right answer?

Finally Hear Her Voice

A baseball game is at commercial break. Jeffrey turns his head to look at the garage. The garage is a representation of a girl he is dating, "Rose." He thinks about her beauty, personality, and whole existence on Earth.

Keep in mind Jeffrey is Schizophrenic. The garage opens, meaning Rose is awaiting his communication. When this happens, he looks forward to getting ahold of her on his cellphone. There are so many ways to get in contact with her. All he must do is pick and choose an option.

Jeffrey looks forward to conversing with Rose. She seems excited to talk to him. It is nice to have someone to care for in life. It is also nice when the other person reciprocates.

The first long-term, girlfriend-boyfriend relationship Jeffrey had was a learning experience. It lasted about five years. She and her family cared for Jeffrey, dearly. Toward the end, they both knew it was time to end the relationship.

Now, Jeffrey is happy to be with Rose for a never-ending time. The laughter and joyful smile cheers and glorifies his happiness to be alive. She does not hold back when laughing at crazy yet simplistic occurrences.

Spending time with her in the hospital was misleading at first. Rose was quiet and kept to herself. You could tell she was disgusted by the other girls in group. The way Rose eyed them when they spoke, Jeffrey thought she was going to argue with someone.

She finally started yelling her opinion and cried out loud. This was a different side Jeffrey had not seen. Through her actions, Jeffrey never thought he and Rose had anything in common.

Did the yelling and screaming make Jeffrey curious?

Fishing

Taste the fish frying in a pan
We are doing everything we can
Feelin' it with my hand
Please lure, don't hit the sand

My friend gives me a call
I feel really tall
He shows up in my backyard
Heads to the boat and decides to show off
He feels his strong line
Casts it perfect with a lure skirt
Catches his biggest fish
Does an incredible fishing trick
Tells me how to use his lures
Runs around the badass boat
Feel a bite on my bait
Pull it into the side of the ride
My pole bends real hard
Fish is fighting till I retire
Jump around the bass boat
Almost fall in and start to float
Bigass bass finally looks at me
Oh my gosh, is it a he or she?

Reach my hand and pinch its lip
Pull it in with a nice big grip

Taste the fish frying in a pan
We are doing everything we can
Feelin' it with my hand
Please lure don't hit the sand

He doesn't believe in keeping his catch
Feel bad for mentioning it
Sports fishing is his thing
Making it do a fish wheelie
Fishing
He is a fishing god
Never will lose his reel or rod
Respecting each other's stuff
We make a good combo

Chorus:
Taste the fish frying in a pan
We are doing everything we can
Feelin' it with my hand
Please lure don't hit the sand
Please lure don't hit the sand
Please lure don't hit the sand

Flowers for Sigrid

When my mom passed
I was sad
She went through pain
I think she was glad
We traveled the world and
The United States
We did so much
I forgot the dates
I have a picture of
Me and her
I was so young and
It wasn't a blur
She fought real hard but
Was very tough
Ate chips of ice and
Had enough
Her head was bald
Because of the virus
She stood very tall and
Did not fuss
I will remember
All the days
We sat together

In the sunrays
When I go to her burial
I think good thoughts
At the same time
My stomach has knots
Accept the flowers
That I give you
Sigrid your son
Believes in you true.

Food Inside Stasher's Mouth

Two-year-old puppy, "Dragster," is wearing silver metal spikes attached to a black collar. His hair is white with black spots. The pit bull is energetic and looks forward to road trips. Jeffrey thinks pit bulls are mean because of television documentaries and specials. The dogs fitting this description are nice in the animal shelter where Jeffrey used to volunteer.

At Rose's home, Dragster rushes up to you and is super hyper. The dog runs around the living room, jumping on couches and people. Dragster is disciplined when traveling on vehicle adventures. He is just a puppy.

The seatbelt is pulled through the dog's harness, so Jeffrey, Rose, and Dragster are safe. Sometimes, Jeffrey turns his head to see how his little spotted friend is doing in the backseat. Dragster lays down and glances at Jeffrey.

The three arrive at their destination. Rose unbuckles the dog's seatbelt with a leash on. She takes Dragster for a restroom break. Jeffrey forgot to ask Rosearooni, or Rose, for a pet hair remover. It is okay, though. The dog was going to lay in the backseat, yet again.

Four hours go by, Jeffrey and Rose finish setting up the campsite, eating, and playing games. She walks Dragster a short distance and lets the dog wander with the leash on.

The dog runs around the corner. Rose isn't present to hold the animal's restraint.

Tracking a squirrel up a tree, the pup has it surrounded. The stasher or squirrel jumps from branch to branch. Spikes rotate around the tree and create a very strong rotary force.

Eyes on the squirrel are hypnotized with imaginary red spiral rings. The pack rat sits there and breathes quickly and heavily.

The squirrel falls back in its nest facing up in neutral thought mode thinking, *Boy was I lucky*.

Is it that difficult for a stasher to get food?

Friends with an Ex

Jeffrey and Rose ended their relationship for good. He is worried about her well-being. Recently, she was diagnosed Schizophrenic. Jeffrey visits his psychologist. The doctor asks if Jeffrey can be friends with her. Jeffrey thinks he might be able to have a friendship bond after the breakup.

Jeffrey tends to undergo deep feelings. Becoming friends with his ex-girlfriend might be okay. He has male friends that become friends with their exes. Jeffrey does not know how they do it without emotions overtaking their heart.

He visualizes a super model dressed up like Rose. She is very beautiful and smart. Spending time with her is a tremendous experience. If they cook in the future, would a friendship subsist amongst other factors?

Jeffrey walks past his old apartment with his friend. He looks at the porch and window blinds that are cracked open. Many memories surface. Jeffrey writes most of his short stories and poems in the breathable space. He even plays his musical instruments from time to time.

Pregnancy is the main topic. Rose mentions vomiting around the same time every day. She says she would raise the baby. Jeffrey has no idea if this is true or not. The first time they took the pregnancy test, the results were negative.

Jeffrey says he wants to take care of the baby, too. His psychologist seems to think it is stress from the breakup that is prolonging her period.

His friends from Lake Conroe visit Jeffrey to see his new living arrangements in the woods. They come to see how he is feeling. They heard about Jeffrey's breakup. Jeffrey believes they came over to support him.

Jeffrey has been searching for answers about Rose. His medication is working properly. Jeffrey will always wonder.

Was Rose the super model, Rise Above, and is she pregnant with Jeffrey's child?

Fungus

We look at the sea
On the side there is a tree
The tree is dark and wet
On the side is a fishing net
We sit down on a rock
In the water is a dock
We walk down to the end
The girl starts to bend
Setting up a picnic spot
In the cooler is a lot
Looking each other in the eyes
The girl's cheeks start to rise
Her smile is so big
She reaches down and starts to dig
Grabbing the food
She is never rude
Both of us make a plate
Food is so good that we rate
Our legs hanging over the edge
Swinging to splashes on the sea ledge
I will not regret
Singing about the net

Till the time comes
Let's be beach bums.

God's Wish

The first and last time they saw each other was in a restaurant but were separated. Jeffrey was going to approach her in the cafeteria. The fire alarm went off, and he could not introduce himself. People were rushing out of the restaurant, forcing her to be pushed out of the door. Falling on the ground, she had a concussion.

Jeffrey begged to ride in the ambulance with her but could not. Paramedics said family members only. Her name could not be released either. He thought he would never see her again.

Splish, splash, splish, splash!

Jeffrey storms through the water-tipped waves. Air gushing past boots and jeans. Jeans and shirt flapping so hard as if he was skydiving vertically.

Flooded water climbs another half-foot distance. The whole area becomes a huge pond. Fish and ducks race around his Wellington boots and water splashes a little on his jeans. Jeffrey has fish and duck food in his pockets. Food is thrown so far that the animals sprint in desperate measures. Now, Jeffrey is on his way in an even more serious manner.

Thighs burn and knees bend creating dirt-eroded boundaries. Striving to attain his mad, intense destination, his hair finally settles in silent peace. He reaches her.

She looks in Jeffrey's eyes, a light drizzle starts with slight thunder and lightning. They do not run under the canopy behind her to take cover.

She says with a sweet and innocent voice, "I'm glad I woke up from my coma today...I love you! What is your name?"

He whispers, "Jeffrey. You are all I think about. I remember the way we looked at each other in the restaurant. What is your name?"

"My name is Rose. I saw you while I was under. You were wearing a blue t-shirt, blue and white pajama bottoms, and a necklace with a white face."

Jeffrey pulls out his necklace, "Is this the necklace?"

"Yes."

"It is called a Moon Face. I love looking at the moon, so I made a necklace."

"It is beautiful, Jeffrey. At the end of my coma, a Moon Face necklace was wrapped around my neck in my mind."

She lifts hands and arms to reach around his body. Jeffrey lifts his, too. They hug for five minutes. Cheeks rub and press against one another. Crying and squeezing hard. Tears are forced toward their lips leaving a salty flavor in the mouth.

Why was Rose wearing a Moon Face necklace in her coma?

Going Back to See

Jeffrey was admitted to West Park Springs Psychiatric Hospital after spending his last day in Willis, Texas. Schizoaffective Disorder took over. That was the last day he drank alcohol and smoked marijuana.

Jeffrey cannot explain why he quit both habits. You are not allowed to do either habit in the hospital. After spending time in West Park Springs Psychiatric Hospital, Jeffrey went to Cypress Creek Hospital Outpatient Care for therapy. This was the best therapy Jeffrey received in his life.

He smoked at least two cigarettes during the "fresh-air breaks." Other patients smoked with him. They conversed, smoked, and had a great time getting to know each other.

Jeffrey started working out toward the end of his stay at Cypress Creek. A man approached him one day. He told Jeffrey that he wanted to lose weight and have a "cut" body. Jeffrey showed him how to work out. Jeffrey then mentioned that he smokes cigarettes. The man changed Jeffrey's life.

The gent worked at a gas station and mentioned a certain type of vape. Jeffrey bought the "Vuse" right away. Jeffrey had tried over and over to quit smoking. The "Vuse" was the solution that kicked cigarette smoking.

"Blu" was another product, which weaned him off nicotine concentration. Pretty soon, Jeffrey will be down to zero percent nicotine concentration. His family is extremely proud of this achievement.

After Jeffrey's stay at his most recent apartment, he dated Rose. Both have been remarkable influences around each other. Jeffrey's family can tell he is on target, medically and emotionally. They do not understand why Jeffrey and Rose break up and get back together all the time. Jeffrey believes Schizoaffective Disorder is a dominant factor.

Jeffrey's dad said he could get together with his friends from Willis, Texas. He asked that Jeffrey not see anybody that still partied. Jeffrey's first friend that he saw had a drink in his hand. His friend asked if it was okay if he smoked some marijuana. Jeffrey did not mind. His Schizoaffective Disorder was telling him that marijuana usage was legal in the state of Texas.

Jeffrey bumped into his friend's mother on the way to the backyard. She never had clothes on. Just a t-shirt, hat, and something underneath the shirt. Her husband laid on the bed watching television. Jeffrey walked outside after his friend.

His friend busted out the pipe to smoke marijuana. A pack of cigarettes lay on the chair to his left. His friend basically did one habit after the other. This did not bother Jeffrey. Jeffrey pulled out his "Blu" and inhaled a few times. Deep down. He did not require the vape but drew in the vapor, anyway.

They talked to a good friend on FaceTime, fished, and went to a bar/restaurant where another friend was located.

Jeffrey ate food at the bar/restaurant. His friend ordered drink after drink.

Jeffrey asked his friend if he felt drunk at all. The friend said he did not feel intoxicated. Jeffrey asked why he drank if it did not give him a high. Jeffrey's friend kind of agreed with Jeffrey.

Jeffrey's lake friends will always be great friends. One is making straight "*A*s" at a university. Two others moved to attend school. Finally, another one has three jobs and is supporting three children.

Jeffrey will always care for these friends. He just wants the best for them. All of them were close for at least eight years. Hopefully, they understand Jeffrey's mental disorder.

How often will Jeffrey see his lake friends?

Habitual Rain

Food starts to boil and steam while sitting in an area in between others. Safety does not exist except for the tackle box in the car.

Sitting down in comfort and surviving odd and even natures, the leaves and grass move with unexpected fluency.

The grill fire hits medium charcoal burn with glowing fortitude. A wet drizzle falls on her hair which is beautifully strung together.

Precipitation falls a little harder, driving the girl for cover while Jeffrey covers the deliciously marinated meat and saucy potatoes.

Before this, Jeffrey was in a mental hospital because of his Schizophrenia. A great deal was going through his mind. Other patients were not who he thought they were. He believed celebrities were dressing up as outpatients to mess with his mind.

A beautiful girl named "Haley" reminded Jeffrey of a super model, "Rise Above." She did not look like Rise one bit, but her personality and body reminded Jeffrey of the model. Jeffrey and Haley got to know each other very well.

During "fresh-air breaks," they would joke around with one another; teasing and flirting. She was married, so

Jeffrey did not cross that boundary. He was a little standoffish.

Patients around him were kicking chairs when Haley and Jeffrey were next to each other. Jeffrey wanted it to be the truth but felt those were *crazy beliefs.*

One day, sitting outside on the wooden bench covered by a canopy, Jeffrey mentioned that the *Medical Field* is making progress on individuals bearing Autism. An Autistic patient ran toward them and sat down. He looked around, and it started to rain within the surrounding area.

Jeffrey looked at the rain in awe and wondered, *is this Rise sitting next to me? Is some kind of spirit trying to send us a message? Are we soulmates?*

Why does it rain when they are together?

Heartfelt Change

Rose's mom, Rose, and Jeffrey make a road trip to help Sue move away from her soon to be ex-husband.

Rose wakes me up from a nap at Sue's house. Lacking sleep from the night before, eyes are bloodshot from the best nap ever.

Jeffrey walks outside toward the vehicle and notices all the boxes they loaded without him. He is very thankful yet feels a little guilty that the boxes were packed without him.

Sue's dog is taking a turn in life. Jeffrey's girlfriend loads him in the back of the vehicle. She buckles him in through the harness attached to his body.

Jeffrey has a hunch. He thinks a random car that pulled up is her soon to be ex-husband. It is.

Will they renew their feelings for each other?

His Dream Girl

Ryan Gosling and Emma Stone looked at each other in the eyes at the end of the movie *La La Land*.

Jeffrey Andrew, who has strong feelings for Rise Above, tells himself that he will look at Rise like that every day if he is married to her.

It amazes Jeffrey how *La La Land* is comparable to his romantic feelings for Rise Above. He pictures dancing with her all the time, holding her hand, driving in a car with her, playing music around her, and many other things.

Jeffrey Andrew's dad says Jeffrey can relate to the movie. Jeffrey thinks it will be an action or mystery movie, but *La La Land* portrays his daydreams of Rise.

Mr. Jeffrey Andrew is looking through a random magazine. He runs into a modeling section of the magazine. Jeffrey sees a picture of Rise Above and thinks she is perfect for him. He notices she is single in her documentary.

Is Rise Above everything he dreams of?

I Hope Not

Sweaty hair is flying because bike pedals go faster above the trail. Adjusting the handlebar mirror, the fella turns the front wheel forty-five degrees, jerks it back-and-forth, and tries to obtain composure.

Jeffrey sees his girlfriend with no helmet because coolness comes before safety in her eyes. Rose does not want to mess up her hair. This throws off the safety concept. She can hurt herself without the helmet.

Jeffrey tells his woman how to engage the brakes. Comprehension does not exist because other things cross her brain. Trees and grass pass by at a rapid speed. Jeffrey is really worried about her safety now.

Traveling at full speed, the couple tilt to the left to make it around the curve. Brakes are a necessity for this trail. She reaches the ground with her rubber-soled tennis shoes to prevent a collision with some random people.

Jeffrey stops with eyes wide open. Rose does not remember where the brakes are located on the handlebar. Rose approaches the group and swerves to the right. Fortunately, Rose slows down like she is jogging on a bicycle. The lady comes to a complete stop and looks at Jeffrey.

Jeffrey knew the bicycle experience would be dangerous but does not complain. He asks her if she wants some water. Rose walks to Jeffrey with the bike between the legs. She tells him he does not stay close to her when riding. Deep down Jeffrey feels safer giving Rose space.

Does Jeffrey have a good gut feeling about Rose hurting herself?

Icy Physique

It's cold outside and a fire is SAFELY prepared in the fireplace. Snowflakes fall slowly on the lawn and deck. Jeffrey has his hiking boots on. Walking and leaving his footprints everywhere, he has to be careful not to slip on the deck.

It hardly snows in the area. Usually, it does not snow very long. Jeffrey takes advantage of the weather. Snowballs are placed in the freezer for a later time. He is going to blast his friends with the snowballs, and they would not be prepared for the snow attack.

Jeffrey's friend texts him. His buddy is arriving in ten minutes according to Google Maps. Jeffrey loads his big cooler with snowball after snowball. He waits behind the wooden fence for his pal to arrive. Jeffrey hears his friend's car from one-hundred yards away.

Jeffrey's pal sees the snowball in his throwing hand. Jeffrey's right hand throws the large, white ball of ice toward his friend. Jeffrey's pal is behind his car door, avoiding the white, icy blob. The window is rolled down a little. The snowball breaks into pieces and sneaks by the door window. Jeffrey's friend is covered in snow.

Inside the lakehouse is a three-logged stack of firewood. Both ends of the starter log are lit and flames spread to the middle.

The flame is monstrous, swaying all over the place, trying to sweep around the other two pieces of wood. The flare starts to flicker everywhere. Especially around the sparing pieces of firewood.

Jeffrey kneels rubbing his hands together, trying to get warm. Icicle, hanging down like a stalactite, melts from one of his nostrils, hitting the brick surface in front of him. His whole body is red even though he is dressed warm.

Starting a SAFE fire is an easy task.

How do human beings adapt to weather where they live?

Imaginary Girlfriend

Woke up in my chair
Was a problem with my hair
Brushed it back with my fingers
Put my hat on my head
Tiptoed to the deck
I said what the heck
Took a breath of the wind
Vision started to bend
Wish my girl was with me
We had a little tea
Saw her smile with one breath
Was impressed and almost saw death
We grabbed a rod and reel
Sunburns started to peel
Hands got close and started to feel
I almost started to kneel (Like I'm gonna propose)
I watched her cast her line
Couldn't help it, I looked at her behind
She was good with her bait
Pulled in a nice take
Her hair started to curl
Wish I could give her a pearl
She wasn't like that

She would appreciate a piece of grass
I casted my fishing line
Our lines started to intertwine
She undid the fishing knot and
Smiled at me a whole lot
I'm gonna miss her soft skin
Appreciate her way deep within
I don't want to drop my pencil
Bye bye, my imaginary friend.

Involuntary Goals

Jeffrey receives a text message from Rose. She missed "National hug a drummer day." Jeffrey plays various instruments. Playing a drum set is one of the select instruments.

Rose makes Jeffrey laugh when she talks about national days. Cheeseburgers and hotdogs were the last national celebrations. She takes the festivities serious but in a cute manner.

They start hanging out again. Both have the same schedule and are good friends. Jeffrey thinks it is nice to see Rose. She is knowledgeable and computer savvy. Jeffrey has never met an intellectual and attractive woman like her.

He is in love with her pretty eyes. They shine from across the room. Jeffrey has not told her but will one day. Rose has a lot going for her. Jeffrey points it out, so she will do something incredible with her life.

Jeffrey finds out that Rose can write. She wrote and edited her first novel. Now, she is writing three novels, simultaneously. Jeffrey enjoys writing his short stories. They get together and write on the leather couch with their laptops.

Jeffrey never found himself interested in creating stories. His mind works different because of his

Schizoaffective Disorder diagnosis. Jeffrey wrote a few poems. He is in the middle of writing a song to one of the poetries.

Will Rose enjoy the song?

Love Until the End

Stroking a person by the soft cheek
True emotion is what I seek
Sometimes it is hard to close my eyes
I like to squeeze slowly between your thighs
We touch fingers and clasp our hands shut
She has a cute butt
We hug hard before we die
Our relationship isn't a lie
I feel your passion and belief
Believing in me and my faith
Whatever it is I will know
Wherever it is I will go
Spending time always with you
Feeding a family of two or a few
I look at you till that day
Only with you I will stay.

Maybe

Jeffrey receives a phone ring while talking to Dad. It is his ex-girlfriend, Rose. Her medicine plus other material items need to be picked up.

Jeffrey's neighbors walk around the apartment complex every day. Different scenarios have random meaning.

A couple would walk in Jeffrey's view with a child. This means Rose has a child with a father. Jeffrey has not met or seen the imaginary father. Jeffrey asks Rose if she has a child, but she says "No" every time. He alleges she is lying.

The psychologist suggests Jeffrey should be honest with Rose; ask personal, psychotic questions over and over so there is clarity. The same goes with people who love or care about him. Jeffrey still has little mishaps. He does not know if Rose's mother understands his psychosis.

Her mom drove Rose to Jeffrey's, and he wasn't sure if her mom would be upset. Rose's mother is a little old-fashioned. Jeffrey has to watch where he is looking, or the mother will think he is eyeing other women.

Jeffrey asks his dad about the situation. He says Jeffrey's mom and stepmom got on his case about looking at other females. Jeffrey never experienced this with girlfriends in the past. The situation is in Jeffrey's mind.

This might have led to the break-up. Things were going great until Rose brought up that super model, "Rise Above," the night before.

Upon arrival, Jeffrey grabs her purple blanket, black socks, medicine, and other significant belongings. Rose does not look upset to Jeffrey. Maybe she is over him.

Did the Schizophrenia delusions screw up this bonding relationship again?

Meeting Sue

Conversations held on her cellphone sounded stimulating. Rose had thought-provoking conversations with her older sister.

Jeffrey could hear Sue's voice on Rose's cellphone speakers, either turned up or she spoke loud. Conversations were coherent and a closeness existed.

Rose said they looked like twins. Can't wait to see her imaginary image. Meeting Rose's older sister "Sue" for the first time should be interesting.

Each member of the family is introduced at separate times. This encounter will bring Rose's mentality and the way she exemplifies family traits.

Will Jeffrey like "Sue"?

Mixed Tapes

Walking to the bedroom after a shower when Jeffrey was young. His bedroom was the destination.

Record/cassette/radio/stereo was turned on to be played. Jeffrey loved music played on radio stations and made mixed tapes all the time.

Hitting record/play at the same time not to miss a beat played on reception radio stations is how mixed tapes were made.

Jeffrey would write down the band/song titles on the provided cassette paper. This was provided in cassette cases. He was bad with band and song names, so he had to listen quick and hard to the broadcasting DJ.

Is this how music initially became a part of Jeffrey's life?

Musical Blood Waves

Jeffrey sits on his drum throne and admires the colored lights around him. Laser lights shine too.

Blink, blink, blink.

There is a disco ball hanging from the ceiling and spinning at a steady speed. Two strong white lights shine on the mirror ball to give it a party effect.

Dizziness, sweat, and a need for deep musical sex fills Jeffrey's passionate thoughts as the melody enters his viewpoint. Music rushes through Jeffrey's body as if falling to his toes till the last little breath.

Screams, whispers, and longings from the audience unite Jeffrey with the limbs attaching fortitude and outburst. A rage overcomes his soul when it is loud or quiet.

Jeffrey fights and fights while colleagues drain themselves with the same fury. Their exertions are dissimilar from his. Playing diverse instruments is a variable that can't be defined.

Jumping, bouncing, swaying, lifting, slamming, grabbing, holding, falling, kicking, and driving our spirits to points that are understood!

A song ends, and glass breaks in the background.

Will this numbness conquer Jeffrey's interior, again?

No Way Out

There is no way out; Jeffrey looks back and forth. His girlfriend watches his eyes figure out a never-ending story.

Trees, grass, and dirt subdue and force a concentrated vision to bend and wrap around curves leading to a place far away. A dirt road shocks Jeffrey, since he is going ten miles over the speed limit on winding roads.

Exhaust, fumes, brakes, and a gas pedal tempt the vehicle into a map of colors drawn on a table with map pencils. Are they sharpened or bold?

Are their cellphones working?

The music is high as Jeffrey and Rose evacuate the main road. Hills smooth because the tires grip tightly to the sensitive friction. Dust kicks up after the vehicle climbs and descends through the wavy trail. There is no place to make a two-point turn.

Finally, a dirt intersection is awaiting their arrival. He looks at his compass. Jeffrey asks Rose if she wants to go north, west, or east.

"West sounds like a good direction," she says. In about a mile, a small body of water is in sight.

Jeffrey stops the automobile and sees branches, which can be removed by hand. He puts his vape in his right front pocket, unplugs the cellphone, and opens the vehicle door. The back left pocket is a great place to put his phone.

Then, he walks quickly to let his girlfriend out of the vehicle. Rose waits. She is so cute, waiting for Jeffrey to let her out of the automobile every time. Jeffrey always looks forward to the soft and gentle kisses.

Instead of grabbing the cooler backpack, Jeffrey walks in front of Rose to seek out the situation. He figures it would take three or four grabs to clear a parking spot. Jeffrey tells Rose to stay outside while he parks the vehicle.

There is a lot of space, and it is easy to drive into his manmade parking spot. Jeffrey loves these types of experiences. Rose is up for anything, too. Luckily his tent, his and her fishing poles, tackle box, picnic blanket, black backpack, and cooler backpack are in his automobile.

Both set up the tent, walk toward the water with fishing poles in hand, and fish for catfish. They put plastic worms on fishing hooks, which are tied onto the fishing line. Bobbers float patiently on the surface of the water after casting the bait.

Rose's bobber sinks into the water. She pulls hard on her pole. The fish is under water swimming in all directions. Jeffrey gazes at her as she reels and fights the fish. She catches their first catfish. As time evolves, they catch five catfish. It is time to clean the fish with a fillet knife. Jeffrey grabs the fish stringer and they gut catfish one by one.

Rose cleans the last catfish, and Jeffrey gathers firewood to cook and have a romantic dinner by the fire. Aluminum foil is wrapped around the bamboo skewers, which have chunks of catfish on them. It turns out to be a delicious dinner.

Jeffrey throws more firewood on the campfire. They take eleven steps back, unzip the tent, step in the tent, and zip it back up. The two hold each other as they watch the fire burn. As the fire burns down, Rose becomes sleepy. Jeffrey and Rose lay down and fall asleep.

Next day, the two load Jeffrey's vehicle and head east.

Will this ever happen, again?

Paresthesia

Looking down at grass-infested dirt, turning left or right might lead to fishing, eating, or warming up. They hang two trash bags in the air to prevent unwanted animals from coming to their campsite; one for recycling and the other for trash.

This is the first time Jeffrey uses his camping tent. He and his girlfriend, Rose, are time efficient when they assemble the tent. They lay it flat on the ground, slide the tent poles diagonally across the tent, lift it up, and knock stakes in the ground with a rock. This holds the tent in place. A waterproof roof is attached on top of the tent just in case it rains.

Inside the blue and white cooler are drinks and food that they brought from home. Ice is purchased at the entrance of the campground.

They sit down at the picnic table, which is located in between Jeffrey's vehicle and the recycle/trash bags. They take two sandwiches and drinks out of the blue and white cooler. Cheer with the vapes as to appreciate what they have accomplished so far.

Lunch is finished, and it is game time. Jeffrey uses the dominoes' container to hold his dominoes. He cannot believe how Rose holds her dominoes with two hands. The instruction manual is placed on the rough-surfaced, concrete picnic table. The dominoes do not get scratched.

They play "Speed" and "Crazy Eights" with a deck of cards next. Jeffrey has a hard time picking up the cards quickly because of the surface they provide. Rose does not have any problems. After that, Jeffrey puts the blue and white cooler next to the roof cord, so they will not trip on it at night.

Daylight is one of Jeffrey's main concerns as the sun sets in the distance. He tries to memorize the location of the blue and white cooler, backpack cooler, dominoes and cards' backpack, fire pit/grill, picnic table, trash bags, water faucet, tent, neighbors, and automobile.

Standing still, little creatures crawl and bite Jeffrey's legs all over. Paresthesia takes over and eliminates any kind of pain. He looks and slowly washes them off. The animal ants paddle out of the faucet-created pond looking for their next purpose.

Headlamp strapped on the forehead changes moods that are becoming. Light is bright, medium, and low, red or white. Jeffrey's head turns and discovers the charcoal fire before it rains. Red light is inexplicable when directed toward the charcoal fire. Coals have an evil presence.

Legs stretch one after the other to cook a meal. Food is on the fire pit/grill.

It drizzles.

Jeffrey senses a lightning storm. Tearing off the first piece of grilling aluminum foil from the package, Jeffrey covers the cheese-sauced gratin potatoes which start to boil. Rain comes down harder and lightning is everywhere. He flips the steaks. Jeffrey tears this piece quicker, wrapping it around the top boundaries of the steaks. The steaks are cooking very well.

He goes in the tent to meet his girlfriend. Jeffrey makes her feel relaxed and tension free. The rain does not come down too hard. Jeffrey tells Rose to stay in the tent while he manages the food on the grill.

Headlamp is wrapped around his Astros baseball cap, adjusted to the brightest setting. Jeffrey walks quickly to the grill and checks the food. It looks perfect. He grabs food in the grilling aluminum foil and brings it in the tent.

A lantern lights up the tent. He pulls off the foil, and Rose's eyes look very impressed. They use plastic forks to eat the potatoes and the steaks with their hands. The two converse while eating and listening to music.

Also, the blue and white cooler has ice cream cones, marshmallows, and Hershey's chocolate bars. Rose shows Jeffrey how to make S'mores in a different way. She stuffs the cones with chocolate and marshmallows, wraps aluminum foil around the S'mores, and puts them on the grill. It starts to rain again. They leave dessert on the grill and hang out in the tent. Ice cream cones toast perfectly, marshmallows and Hershey's melt dreamily.

They fall asleep on the pillows and cushions.

What will they do tomorrow?

Parents

There's a picture Jeffrey has seen before. It's a picture of his dad holding him on the beach in Galveston. Jeffrey's brother, sister, and mother are there too. His dad was a different person.

When you hear that you are having a child, both parents get excited and experience joy. As time sits in, the dad and mother want the best for their child.

Receiving your driver's license for the first time is fun. After you graduate from high school, it is still fun to drive your vehicle. When Jeffrey graduated from college, his driver's license served a different purpose, the money-making world.

Our parents get dressed in the morning, drive in traffic, and finally make it to their place of business. When Jeffrey made it to the office, he was exhausted.

Parents work all day; drive back home, try to put a smile on their face when they get to the house to see their families. They want the best for their spouse and children. The stress tends to push the parents in different directions.

DO NOT do what Jeffrey did! Talk to your parents like they are your friend. It's not too late.

Jeffrey thinks our parents forget the time they got married, the way they stared at each other…smiled at each other…and maybe cried a little.

Jeffrey thinks you should have or adopt a child when you find someone you are truly in love with, married to, or if you are a single adult.

Is life about this endless cycle?

Psychologist

As Jeffrey approaches the house, he finds it creepy and mysterious. He enters the premises. A stale mist drifts past his nose as his psychologist shakes his hand. Dimness perceives Jeffrey's magnified vision and he feels like he is inside a Stephen King novel.

The psychologist offers Jeffrey bottled water, but Jeffrey suspects unknown secrets beyond the refrigerator. He accepts the bottled water, which is sealed shut with the plastic lid.

Jeffrey looks the psychologist up and down to see if he is dressed professionally. Jeffrey sits on the black leather couch with water in hand, and they begin their session.

Jeffrey scopes out the backyard, briefly. The psychologist's pool is full of algae and consists of different types of fish. Jeffrey says he should "shock" the pool a few times to be humorous. This will enable the doctor to swim in it. Also, an empty hot tub is in a gazebo which will cost too much money to make it function. The psychologist likes to save his money and disagrees with Jeffrey.

They sit and converse about Jeffrey's Schizoaffective Disorder. Jeffrey opens by mentioning his girlfriend, Rose.

Rose's hallucinations and delusions have transpired into evil fictitious realities. These imaginary people are telling her to do certain actions. Her anti-psychotic medication is very important, and Jeffrey believes her psychiatrist has not prescribed the correct dosage.

The fictional images are telling her not to take her medication. They do not want to be rid of Rose's thought processes. Sometimes, they want her to choke herself, so the medication will not travel through her body. She also fancies Jeffrey swinging from the bedroom fan in the middle of the night. The delusions and hallucinations are getting worse and worse. Rose might have to go to the hospital, according to Jeffrey's psychologist.

Jeffrey has been concerned for quite some time. Jeffrey, Rose, and her mother are meeting with a new psychiatrist. They will see what happens next.

Will Rose overcome the hallucinations, visions, images, and delusions?

Rise Above Is Her Name

Rise Above is her name, and Jeffrey Andrew finds himself at home in Willis, Texas.

Jeffrey's backyard consists of a lake, grass, and rocks leading to the water. Out of the blue, he is on Facebook and receives a notification from a girl named Lola. He has no idea who she is but cannot believe she mentioned her friend's name, Rise Above.

The only reason Jeffrey knows this girl is because he randomly noticed her in a magazine one day. Mr. Andrew saw the beautiful, blonde, blue-eyed girl, and it was mentioned she was a single super model. That poked his attention.

Now Jeffrey doesn't usually look up girls in magazines and wants to date or maybe marry them, but there is something about Rise. She seems joyful and full of life.

Lola tells him in the notifications, "Rise will find things for you to do."

She is saying that Jeffrey wouldn't be bored if he ever dated Rise Above.

Then, Mr. Andrew feels like Rise's friends are getting involved. There are celebrities Jeffrey is familiar with; a friend of a friend, and many others trying to hint that she might be interested in him.

Jeffrey's friend gives him a Maxim Magazine with Rise Above on the cover. She looks beautiful and exotic. Jeffrey thinks that is another hint that she likes him.

One of Rise's friends asks Jeffrey Andrew to write a guitar song for her. He writes the lyrics like it is a novel or rap song. Jeffrey can't stop shooting the words out of his mouth when he writes it initially. Jeffrey's vocal teacher asks him to shorten it, which he does.

Jeffrey Andrew has written and recorded songs in the past. This song took him the longest because emotions took over his singing ability. Jeffrey couldn't even say "Yes" or "No" to his vocal teacher because crying was a possibility. All he could do was nod his head back and forth or up and down.

Will Jeffrey ever meet the beautiful, blue-eyed, blonde sweet girl?

Romantic Relationship

Two silver faces are next to each other in flight, rectangular in shape. Only a single eye pokes out finding the way to space-warped speed. Each silver face has a retina with the same diameter. The two are almost considered identical twins. They calculate, light up, and think alike.

External hard drives are attached to the bodies through USB ports. The drives lay on each other as if holding hands. Heat grows as time progresses. Love and adoration for one another makes hands warm and develop a pulse.

Power is plugged in to give ultimate performance. They ask each other for coordinates at super speed. Nobody understands their lingo except for the two.

The silver faces talk to each other romantically. They even cook with updates, downloads, and various things. The two know how to communicate well. Their BASIC language mesh.

Do they have the same knowledge?

Rose's First Fish

Jeffrey has to explain to Rose the basic cast with a fishing rod and reel. He is familiarizing himself with this type of fishing reel, too. His casts are not perfect, and they are learning together. Jeffrey enjoys this system.

Three months go by, Jeffrey and Rose get close to their destination. Jeffrey pulls his vehicle over the curb. Then parks in the grass. He gets excited because it is fishing time.

The fishing rods are between them in the front of the SUV. Jeffrey gets out of the driver's side of the vehicle after gathering his belongings. He shuts the door and lets Rose out of the passenger side door. They kiss and walk to the back of the Sports Utility Vehicle. Jeffrey opens the trunk and his fishing tackle box, rods and reels, and backpacks are in his sight.

He pulls out the fishing rods and reels and put them on the ground. Then, he grabs two out of four lure boxes. They might lose a lure or catch a fish. Needle nose pliers may be needed to take a hook out of a fish's mouth.

They walk down one side of the creek wearing relaxed clothes. Jeffrey suggests casting in a certain location. He and Rose walk down the side of the creek casting at numerous spots. They make it back to their starting point.

97

Rose casts. She catches her first fish, ever! Jeffrey watches her pull and tug. The fish is fighting! It is a challenge for her to pull it in. Jeffrey is very happy and ecstatic for Rose! She has been talking about catching a fish for the longest time. Jeffrey feels like her luck is going to change in the future.

Jeffrey shows her how to hold the fish. He grabs the fish with four fingers, leaving enough room for Rose to grab it in the middle of the lip. She pinches the fish with two fingers on the lip. Jeffrey takes a picture with her cellphone. Rose looks very happy in the picture holding the fish.

Will Rose strive to be a serious angler with Jeffrey?

Schizoaffective Disorder

So many people do not understand Jeffrey's mental diagnosis. Schizoaffective Disorder is a combination of Schizophrenia and Bipolar.

Jeffrey Andrew struggles with this type of mental condition. When Jeffrey says struggle, he does not get weighed down and tortured by it. It's a different way of looking at perspectives.

Everything existing around him is considered different. Jeffrey gets Schizophrenic delusions from people. These delusions describe people to him in a semi mysterious way.

Answering questions on certain tests makes Jeffrey reach deep in an ambiguous and unpredictable way. It is as if he looks in a different mental sense to the meaning of life.

Jeffrey does not try. It just happens.

People dig into thoughts trying to reason a direction to natural life or death. Perseverance guides those to happiness but sometimes sadness. No matter how hard you try, some reach a monetary value which is satisfactory in life, and many do not think of life in such a way.

Jeffrey enjoys life in a balanced equilibrium. Love is a major factor. Whether it be a wife, children, family, and/or friendships that understand his illness. Jeffrey has come a long way, since he was nailed later in life by Schizoaffective Disorder.

Mental hospitals have been a part of his life. Jeffrey debates the fact that he has a disorder every day. He looks around to see if people are staring at him and telling him what to think and do by their physical and verbal actions. It is troublesome and mindboggling.

It still exists and overcomes Jeffrey's actions. Jeffrey is feeling much better today. As he types on his laptop, Jeffrey searches for emotion and expression within his brain, trying to define a person who lives. Jeffrey is not empty and lost. He knows people who care for him and he reciprocates. Plus, Jeffrey has always been a positive person.

Jeffrey believes we exist to discover some sort of happiness. For example, music has played a major role in his life. It enhances your willingness to be someone others do not think they can be. People tell Jeffrey they do not have a musical talent. He wonders how they come to that conclusion. Oh well, people pursue something else.

After reading the previous paragraph, "happiness" can be lots of factors in life. The question is which way Jeffrey chooses to go. He chose many avenues in his lifetime and was happy. Jeffrey Andrew is still running strong and will not let Schizoaffective Disorder ruin his life.

Every day at 6:55 PM, Jeffrey's alarm goes off on his cellphone. Jeffrey has a flashlight with a case. The case has a compartment on the side where he stores a quarter. Jeffrey opens the compartment, pulls out the quarter, flips the coin in the air, turns the flashlight on, and flashes it on the coin. Jeffrey says, "It's heads" or "It's tails." Jeffrey looks to see if anyone can hear him after he calls it. Then, he sneaks the quarter and flashlight in the case in an orderly fashion.

Jeffrey is not sure how much money people can bet on the "coin toss." He figures a 50% to 50% chance is an easy way to make money. Jeffrey has been doing this for at least five years that he can recollect. There are days in which he missed the coin toss. But, this to him, it is a form of happiness.

Will he ever receive recognition for anything?

Secrets

Taking care of a person is a desire. You look at each other and find a true definition to their personality. Personality is important to Jeffrey. Can the other person in the relationship carry on a conversation? Are they happy, depressed, outgoing, etcetera? Jeffrey looks for certain characteristics in girls while dating. Dating is fun to Jeffrey because each person is different.

Honesty is key to Jeffrey. He does not want a girl to run back to a guy from the past and cheat on him. Jeffrey is having a hard time with Rose.

Jeffrey being Schizophrenic, believes Rose has a child. He is getting delusions from his neighbors and civilians everywhere he goes. The delusions are horrible. A couple would walk by Jeffrey with a child in a stroller. This meant Jeffrey had a child with Rose. He does not care about Rose having a child, but Jeffrey thinks she is lying about the situation.

When Jeffrey and Rose do not see one another, he believes she is taking care of the baby. Jeffrey also alleges she is bumping into the father of the child on a regular basis, swapping the baby back and forth and hanging out together like they are in a secret relationship. Jeffrey does not want to be a part of a girl's secret relationship.

Finding true love is difficult and cannot reach its true destiny. Lips, eyes, nose, and other features help Jeffrey decipher relationship power.

Longing for a girl is there in perpetual reality but falls from the gray sky to the depths of the Earth's core.

Is there meaning to their hanging out relationship? Are they just hanging out?

Jeffrey finds himself in a couple drifting from one side to the other. Reaching the middle equilibrium of their bond is tough. Will he ever obtain a high bond with a girl?

Sitting next to her and touching her gently, are they reaching certain levels in their relationship? Jeffrey is trying to find the level they are at but is having a hard time. Why cannot Jeffrey describe that level to himself?

Is he betrayed by her life secrets?

Sightless

Her head and blood in the brain moves around so rapidly to stay alive, searching hard and fast for a solution to undefined survival.

She orders a drink from the bartender. Looking around the dim atmosphere; pinball machine, pool tables, cue stick rack, and arcade games are located within the tavern.

Locals sit at their usual seats drinking routine alcoholic beverages. A man sends her a 1.5 fl. oz. shot from across the bar. She knocks it back with no complications. The woman enjoys it so much. She orders herself another one. Bam! Down the hatch.

The lady looks at her watch. It is 2:00 PM central time. Lunch is forgotten. One more person sends her a shot. She is lightheaded with numb thoughts. An additional drink is ordered, and she is out of cash.

Her husband took away her credit cards because she was sneaking away to bars fulfilling her cravings. Jumping from one bar to the next, this was her daily habit. It was breaking her significant other financially and mentally.

He has a full-time job wearing suit and tie. Always worrying about his wife. Calling her is routine. Sometimes she does not answer her cellphone. The lady puts the phone in her expensive purse but ignores the ringtone. This makes him worrisome.

Finally, she answers the cellphone and agrees to come home. It is 5:15 PM central, and she does not recall the time between 2:00 PM and 5:15 PM.

The lady's heart beats fast as obstacles SLAM and KNOCK her off her feet! Hair falls in disarray yet in a feminine sexy twine.

She crawls to her next destination not knowing that a tear falls from the side of her eye. Drips down and splatters so big that it forms a little puddle on the cement.

Earrings act as a sailing mast, taking her across to the other side of the body of water. Luckily, she does not have to exert any energy or will to drown in the tearful seawater.

Will she survive the next destination?

Strutting

Tomorrow is an opportunity for Rose to become someone immense. Her past made an impact on the way she thinks and understands life. Most of those thoughts are cons. Bad things happened to her when she was a child. Now is her chance to grow as an individual, forget about her past, and start a new chapter in life.

She'll walk in a way he's never seen her walk.

Mornings are berserk. Jeffrey's cellphone alarm clock goes off in full volume. Next, his college alarm clock and Rose's cellphone wakes them up.

Jeffrey gets out of bed first, naked or clothed. He arises, making coffee. Rose likes her coffee black. Jeffrey usually puts three ice cubes in the medium-sized coffee cup and stirs it. Bringing the coffee to the bedroom and placing it next to Rose, Jeffrey makes coffee for himself. Not picky in whatever compliments his coffee. He uses whatever is available in the refrigerator or in the cabinet.

Rose strolls out of the bedroom with coffee in hand. Jeffrey gets dressed if naked because they go outside to vape and drink their morning coffee. Clunk coffee mugs after sitting on lounge chairs. They enjoy caffeine and vapes. The two adore getting their day started like that.

Jeffrey and Rose make their way over to her house to get ready for "Torrid Model Search." Glimpsing into the room and closet, loads of laundry and shoes lie on the ground and ridges.

Rose dresses herself in a maroon dress, black stockings, and black belt. She picks out high-heeled, black shoes with silver metal spikes on the back. Jeffrey is attracted to the color and style. Her hair is decked out and fixed fashionably. Jeffrey has never seen this side of Rose.

The Galleria in Houston, Texas, is right around the corner. Rose, her mother, and Jeffrey make a stop in the vehicle. Rose bought makeup at an affordable price on Westheimer.

Traveling through traffic, they drive the lower level of the parking lot and find a great spot. Pulling in, the back end of the automobile sticks out, but they do not think twice about leaving the parking space. Jeffrey takes a picture of the location. Then, the three walk into The Galleria through Neiman Marcus. Jeffrey admires the products in stores and different departments.

Rose's feet start to hurt from the high-heels. A bench is vacant, so she and her mom sit down. Jeffrey goes back to the vehicle and grabs an extra pair of boots. The Timberlands turn Jeffrey on, too. Jeffrey grabs the bag with the boots in it and dashes to Rose and her mother.

If Rose falls and hurts herself, Jeffrey will be worried. Concentrating and walking a sober line in high heels is foregoing. He just wants to see her glee.

People surrounding her might give her GAD (General Anxiety Disorder). Medication is in her possession.

Will she enjoy the experience today?

The Beach

Jeffrey and Rose walk on Galveston beach. The sand washes offshore. Hurricane Harvey floods the area badly.

They develop a sweat from the cloudless sky. Jeffrey suggests walking in the salty water to cool off their feet. Rose gasps for air because her body parts are sensitive. She squeezes Jeffrey's hand to feel his closeness and security. Jeffrey loves her compassion and feminine warmth.

Rose pushes Jeffrey's arm to the right. She wants to get deeper in the water. Waves splash their shins softly, and Rose is startled. She lets out a moan. Rose is close to Jeffrey and can be herself around him. Especially when he caresses her in the fondest way.

Sunlight shines in her eyes as it establishes a beauty never seen by Jeffrey. He pecks her on the lips for five seconds. A second and third peck on her forehead and little nose. She smiles. Jeffrey feels a huge hug from her demonstrating adoration and friendship. Jeffrey loves such a wonderful woman.

They continue to walk in the splashy water. Jeffrey glances at her. He notices a sexy sweat drip down from her forehead to her cheek. They stop. Jeffrey uses his right index finger to dry her off. Rose suggests getting deeper in the salty water. Rose and Jeffrey are the same height, so the water is up to their waists. Rose plummets into the water.

Jeffrey waits for her to rise from the sea. Her hair is incredibly sexy. Jeffrey always loved the wet look on a woman, but this is indescribable. Water drips off Rose's hair, slowly. It seems like slow motion in a movie.

She asks, "Jeffrey, are you going to get yourself wet like I am?"

He replies, "Yes. You make the ocean look refreshing and stimulating."

Jeffrey comes up for air. Rose wipes his hair back and puts her arms around his neck. She kisses him because she cannot resist. Jeffrey kisses her back. It is not a peck this time. Soft, smooth kisses all along their lips define the feelings within their hearts.

Jeffrey asks if Rose wants to bodysurf. They both look back and catch the next wave. They ride a few waves into shore to see who can travel the furthest. Rose is so good at bodysurfing. She beats Jeffrey almost every time. Jeffrey did not know she was so good at riding a wave.

They head back to their belongings on the beach. Rose looks exotic from the water and the way she walks on the sand. They hold hands, tightly, in the amazing breeze.

Rose sits next to Jeffrey on a beach towel. YouTube is turned up on Jeffrey's cellphone. They eat lunch and gaze at each other. Waves crash down twenty-five feet away. Relaxation and ease is present as they gaze at one another.

Will Jeffrey ever get over her eyes?

The Blue Light

Jeffrey sits in the dark wearing blue and white pajama pants and a blue shirt to go with that. A little blue light shines as he stares toward the window with blinds open. Jeffrey inhales, and the light illuminates the room.

He feels his eyes pierce in the direction of the window. Body is blocked by his laptop while sitting on his couch. In deep thought, Jeffrey thinks about the barriers knocking over with imaginary football pads on his shoulders. His lifespan is not routine compared to cyclable life experiences.

While in Europe, Jeffrey has to decide if he is going to pursue music. Jeffrey talks about the trumpet for his five-week stay overseas. He decides to play percussion when he returns to the "Red, White, and Blue."

Two of his neighbors bought drum sets when Jeffrey was in fifth grade. They taught him how to play sixteenth notes on all the equipment. Starting with the snare drum, rack toms, and floor tom, then he added the bass drum and hi-hat. Crash cymbals came last.

It was time to try out for sixth grade band. Jeffrey had to stomp his foot, clap his hands, and hit his thighs for the potential band director. Jeffrey was nervous but pulled it off. A week later, he found out the percussion section would be a part of his life.

Jeffrey did not know what to expect in middle school.

The percussion section was required to buy a bell set, mallets, practice drum pad, and stand. All were stored in a black, sturdy case. Jeffrey toted the case to school and back home every day. It was worth it. Jeffrey still has possession of the casing.

Jeffrey would take percussion practice breaks while studying for school at home. Thirty-minute practices turned into one-hour practices. One-hours' turned into two-hour practices. He could not stop. It was becoming a major part of his life, and Jeffrey loved it.

Jeffrey's percussion instructor pointed out bad habits. He stressed that stick grip was very important. Some of Jeffrey's fellow students stuck their pinkies out when holding the stick. Jeffrey admits it was awkward in the beginning to hold a drumstick. But it is easier to play rhythms when taught the correct way.

It was time for High School Marching Band tryouts.

Jeffrey learned the music required to earn a position to play the snare drum. The snare drum was a prominent instrument to play in drumline. He had to learn how to march to the rhythmic beats, too. Jeffrey played the snare and percussion instruments in high school for four years.

He will never forget the people he met, he thinks as he stares at the blue light.

Will they forget Jeffrey?

The Sand

Jeffrey and Rose end their "more-than-friends" relationship after numerous times. Strong Schizophrenic delusions are taking over mental realities.

Jeffrey races to his car. He brings his "Shakespeare" fishing rod and reel combo along with his tackle box.

The Boy Scout motto is "Be prepared!" so Jeffrey tends to think ahead in everything he executes.

He places the combo in his vehicle; fishing rod tip first, tackle box, and bag full of recyclables next. Jeffrey pulls his cellphone out of the back pocket of his shorts. The baseball cap is low with upside down sunglasses on the visor of the hat.

Jeffrey grabs the handle of the motor vehicle door and rips the door open in an inconspicuous way. None of the neighbors see him leave his apartment and get in his automobile. Right leg first.

It is warm, and Jeffrey shoves the vehicle key perfectly in the ignition without a tremor. After turning on his means of transportation, he is on his suspenseful and mysterious way.

Jeffrey darts around corners and down long streets to avoid the enemy. Schizophrenia kicks in very hard once he is on the streets. Driving! Obviously, the psychiatrist prescribed a low dosage to slow down the delusions in Jeffrey's mind.

Jeffrey drives in different directions because he thinks cars, SUV's, trucks, motorcycles, and eighteen-wheelers are telling him where to drive and when to start and stop vaping. Jeffrey ends up in two major locations.

He does not remember where the first location was, but he thinks he owns the property out there. He pulls up to a gate, which has a lock and the name of the land.

A pond, tons of grass, and three horses are the first three features he comes across. Not one person lets him in the gate, but he thinks he owns the property.

Jeffrey cannot hold back. Tears come to his eyes when he leaves and is on the main road. He thinks he accomplished something on his own, work from past experiences in music, jobs, and school paid off. Self-reflection takes over as he thinks about various achievements. Then, he looks at the "presets" on his radio in his automobile and turns the radio station.

As Jeffrey looks up, cars start talking to him. It is dark and time to eat dinner. He takes a right but pulls into the wrong franchise. A person comes out of the back door of the franchise. He swings his head to the other franchise. Jeffrey goes to the other restaurant.

He waits in the drive-thru. Approaching the pick-up window, he sees the expressions of people that are disappointed in Jeffrey. The delusions are telling him to go inside to eat, but he is not sure.

Jeffrey tells himself mentally, *I can't screw this up!*

He goes inside the Taco Bell and has a few sips of his drink and bites of his food. Schizophrenic delusions tell him to leave right away, so he grabs his food and storms out of the Taco Bell.

He is on to his next destination, "The sand."

Jeffrey follows the instructions the vehicles give him. They lead Jeffrey to a subdivision in which deer walk all over the place. He drives the speed limit and goes under the limit at times to avoid hitting a deer crossing the road.

The car in front of him takes Jeffrey down the quiet, dark, and long road. Jeffrey's car hits a dirt road. He approaches a gate where some people open it for his entry. Jeffrey does not roll down his window and ask questions. He keeps going until another person approaches him in the dark with his truck headlights on. The person rolls his window down, but Jeffrey does not roll down his window to talk to this guy, either. Jeffrey goes right past the gentleman in the truck to, hopefully, meet and greet men in uniform.

Upon arrival, Jeffrey is the only person out there in the wooded area. He thinks a house, or some sort of meeting area, is nearby or within the vicinity. His headlights are still on, but the vehicle is turned off.

Jeffrey looks around at different locations. A pool with picnic tables and bathrooms, a fishing pond with alligators is to the north, and a jungle gym is to the left. Jeffrey thinks he is meeting the super model, Rise Above, to go swimming in the pool.

Jeffrey opens the keypad lock which is supposed to have the key to get into the pool area. The key is not in there. He searches the perimeter but cannot locate the metal solution to open the gate.

Jeffrey jumps in his auto and drives through what used to be a gate. A bump is on the right, but Jeffrey's shocks can handle the rough ride. He cruises at a nice pace so he might see the detailed terrain. Jeffrey comes within reach of a narrow dirt road. He knows this could be characterized as a rollercoaster ride.

When Jeffrey drives on the path, he sees a puddle almost as big as a pond. He backs up quickly. Schizophrenia tells Jeffrey to go for it because his next destination is past the water.

He floors it and forgets to roll up his window. His car zooms through the water and a little water comes in through the driver's side window. He sees sand but doesn't know how deep it is. Jeffrey knows his car is not a four-wheel drive but goes through the sand anyway. His delusions tell him of the prize past the white sand. Jeffrey makes it only about fifteen feet until his back tire digs a hole. He takes his foot off the gas and looks at his food from Taco Bell.

Jeffrey turns the volume up on his automobile radio. It is a rap station. He eats the Taco Bell food and puts the trash in Tupperware because he does not want to attract bugs. The DJ on the rap station says it is time to walk. Jeffrey thinks the DJ is talking to him while stuck in the sand.

Jeffrey gets out of his motor vehicle, stepping into the sand with sandals on a balanced walk. He opens the trunk door and is thankful for the light in the back. Jeffrey can see bugs flying in the air, not too many.

He sprays down his naked body with unscented insect repellant. Then puts clothes back on for his adventure. Jeffrey precedes to the unknown destination. Tackle box, rod and reel, and knife are in his possession to "Be Prepared!"

Jeffrey jogs forward until the path ends, and nobody is out there. There is water on his left, but it is time to turn around and head back to the pool area.

Once again, he jogs for a little while then walks for a short time taking mini breaks. Jeffrey steps on the four-wheeler tracks, which makes it easier to walk and jog with the necessities in his hands. Jeffrey passes his vehicle and backtracks to the puddle. Headlamp is very bright, making it easy to see.

Jeffrey walks around the big puddle on the right side. It is slimy and slippery. He doesn't care. Slamming his sandals into the mud helps tremendously.

The pool is around the corner. He sees the entrance with the bump and starts to jog. Jeffrey makes it back to the pool entrance. Schizophrenic delusions are intense now.

Jeffrey loads one of his tackle box trays with all his bait, hooks, bobbers, weights and everything else inside the other three trays from the tackle box.

He grabs his fish fillet knife and Swiss Army knife, puts those on his belt, which tightens his black and gray camouflage shorts.

Standing straight with fishing combo in hand, his cellphone counts down seventeen minutes. The phone timer might have accidentally been turned on.

Jeffrey finds the perfect landing site. He thinks a helicopter is going to pick him up and take him to the White House.

Seventeen minutes expire, no helicopter. Jeffrey waits an extra five to ten minutes for a ride to the White House, but the Schizophrenic delusions are false. It is time for a long jog and walk.

Jeffrey estimates the jog and walk to be around two miles with full four-tray tackle box and fishing reel and rod. He makes it to a location before the entry gate. The headlamp is positioned toward the sky just in case a helicopter needs a visual. Jeffrey waits there because that spot is perfect for a helicopter landing.

No such luck.

He continues his journey to the gate. Grabbing his cellphone out of his back pocket, the home button is pushed, and the phone lights up in the darkness. Jeffrey swipes his phone on the electronic keypad. Believing it would open the gate and let him off the big acreage, Jeffrey thinks the cellphone is high tech and can break any code.

It does not work.

On the side of the electronic gate is a way out. Jeffrey jumps over the metal bar with fishing equipment in hands. Seen from the distance, it is extremely dark but can see shadows amongst the streets. The dirt road comes to an end, and the road becomes concrete. He is in a subdivision.

Two intersections go by and a strong motored truck pulls into a driveway on the right. The young man gets out of his truck and looks at Jeffrey.

The tackle box is on the ground. Knives are still on the belt. The young man approaches Jeffrey and looks at the tackle suspiciously. He thinks there might be a bomb or gun inside.

Jeffrey asks for a ride home.

The guy decides to ask various questions.

"Where do you live? Why were you back there so long? Did you catch any fish?"

Jeffrey answers those plus many other questions.

Jeffrey asks, "What is your name if you don't mind me asking?"

He says, "Zach."

The young guy goes inside his house. Jeffrey sees him turn on his bedroom lights. Jeffrey plugs in the street intersection on his cellphone while Zach is in his house.

He waits awhile on the street corner and is skeptical about the ride situation. A deer waits by the front door. Jeffrey cannot believe his eyes. Deer are everywhere.

The bedroom light is turned off. Jeffrey thinks Zach is blowing him off. Jeffrey takes a few steps up the long street and notices the front door open. It is Zach walking to his vehicle. Jeffrey meets him at the truck.

Zach asks, "Do you still want a ride?"

Jeffrey exclaims, "Yes! Do you want me to take the knives off my belt?"

Zach says, "No. It's okay."

They put Jeffrey's fishing gear in the back of the truck and drive toward his home.

The truck is warm, and Jeffrey reaches for the switch to open the passenger side window. Zach looks at the action suspiciously.

He says, "I'll open the window."

Zach thinks Jeffrey is grabbing a weapon.

Upon arrival, Zach declares, "I have a gun and was a soldier."

Jeffrey states, "I know. I could tell. Do you want money for gas?"

Zach replies, "No. I just wanted to help out."

Is the super model, Rise Above, waiting for Jeffrey Andrew to pass the water on the left?

The Thorny Bush

Jumping five feet in the air and leaning at a fifteen-degree angle to clear his landing, Jeffrey feels like he is on a pogo stick jumping over bush after bush.

This is his workout. He has springs attached to the soles of his workout shoes and ankle weights wrapped around the bottom of his legs. Bushes look at him because of territorial trespassing. Some bushes are taking a nap but are awakened by the spring-to-ground contact.

They have not had a drink of water in a while and become grouchy. Their hair is getting shaggy, and they need a haircut. Bushes are dependent on property relatives to baby them with food and drinks. It is as if someone abandoned them.

Jeffrey stops at his next bouncing destination. Jeffrey pushes a button, which retracts the springs into his workout shoes. He feels sorry for the bushes. Jeffrey opens his cooler backpack and grabs different types of bottled water. Water is cold and refreshing because of the ice. They smile and thank him as he makes his way to the individual bushes.

There is one more bush. This bush is the tallest and angriest out of the dozen landscaped selection. He is the meanest because thorns are attached to the branches. His name is "Thorny Branch."

Mr. Thorny Branch loves water and mulch but does not like it when strangers feed him. Thorny is very territorial, too.

Mr. Branch frowns in ANGER after realizing something!

Wind blows HARD and fills the shrub's lungs at a magnitude undeniable to humans. The airstream coils down to the base of the plant. The mulch lifts in the air at high intensity.

Mr. Branch deliberately exhales in Jeffrey's direction, forcing hair to spike in mid-air. Hair on Jeffrey's eyebrows shoots straight up his forehead. His goatee has a sponge-like appearance.

Jeffrey asks, "Why did you blow at me in anger?"

The plant yells, "You didn't touch my sharp thorns at the top when attempting to feed me! I am PROUD of my thorns! Don't ever try to nourish me again!!!"

Jeffrey makes it to the other side of Thorny Branch. He looks again at Mr. Thorny Branch disappointedly with his hair straight in the air. Jeffrey does not care for bushes with a negative attitude.

Jeffrey pushes the button on each shoe and springs away from Thorny.

What would happen if Thorny Branch breathes in air and pulls Jeffrey into his sharp thorns?

Unacceptable by Society

Jeffrey and Rose lay in bed talking about their future. Jeffrey thought a super model, "Rise Above," was dressed up as Rose for an unending time.

Jeffrey imagines the super model sliding on an outfit which looks like Rose. Kind of like Halloween.

Rise portrays various people within Jeffrey's life. It is amazing how she changes physical appearances quickly. He does not know how she does it. But Jeffrey thinks Rise is a great actress.

Rose seems to identify with these delusions conquering Jeffrey's mentality. The reason why they are in the same mental hospital discussing problems and difficulties in life.

Both do not believe they will date each other. Jeffrey does not want to cross boundaries, but he does. Staff in the hospital make all patients sign a waiver to protect the mental hospital. Patients cannot touch or even look at one another in flirty or mean ways.

The class has "Family Day," in which patients can invite family members to "Group Discussions." Jeffrey views the class in a different light. He hears about problems patients experience with their family. Now, Jeffrey can put a face with the story.

Many departments exist within the hospital. Besides outpatient care, Jeffrey has experienced inpatient care, meaning admittance over night and daytime to a hospital.

There are other outpatients who attend these "Group" conversations. Mental and physical faults considered by society exist amongst the class. Jeffrey does not consider these to be faults but differences.

Jeffrey has seen diverse behavior in mental hospitals. He believes his is the worst. Memories have deteriorated but some still exist from the deranged behavior. Schizophrenia has taken over Jeffrey's thinking tremendously. Hallucinations and delusions, will he ever get rid of these bizarre thoughts?

Will mental and physical faults ever be accepted by society?

Uncertain Mentality

Head down low in the hospital lobby. Defiance and revenge aren't the sole purpose. Jeffrey just wants to see where it is located.

Police officers eye Jeffrey, who is wearing an Astros baseball cap. He is looking down so nobody can recognize him. It is time to get his cooler backpack, which has a variety of drinks in it. The drinks are, basically, for Rose.

He makes it out to his vehicle and grabs his and Rose's bags. Jeffrey considers the bags a good workout when carrying them, especially during the warm afternoon. Jeffrey makes it back to the lobby. He finishes the Gatorade and waits patiently for his name to be called.

His name is called, and numerous bags are lifted quickly. A race to a solution of unlabeled ends. Doors open and creek shut as walks get faster and faster.

Right is the direction to begin the zigzag. The dead end is incomplete. A recognizable hand is in Jeffrey's vision. It is Rose's mother.

Tracers go back and forth to queue in a target, an end of momentary togetherness. A force field stops humans for check-in liability. Jeffrey ends his zigzag voyage. His girlfriend is inside. Face is expressionless. She is on suicidal watch. Hospital sitters sit at the entrance making sure Rose does not hurt herself.

The Schizophrenia delusions and reality hit Jeffrey at the same time. He does not know what is real.

Sitters tell Jeffrey to unload the cooler backpack in a locker. Jeffrey unloads drinks from the cooler while looking both ways and kneeling. Sitters are suspicious of his actions. He almost does not have room for all the bottled fluids. Jeffrey pushes the remainder in the locker and locks it. You are required to give the key back to one of the hospital sitters and put the bags in the car. Jeffrey, accidentally, keeps the key.

Jeffrey goes inside the room. Rose looks like a zombie. She is Bipolar and suffering from mania. Rose says she might transfer to a mental hospital. He keeps visiting her because he cares for her well-being. Jeffrey stays one night, too.

There is a reclining, old hospital chair. Jeffrey sleeps on the recliner. The hospital sitters give him a blanket and sheet. When Jeffrey wakes up frequently, there is a person watching his every move.

He feels like he is the patient. The staff asks Jeffrey why he has to take medication at 10:00 PM. One of the sitters asks Jeffrey if he is feeling well. Jeffrey fights his hardest to sound sane, speaking properly and not looking around continuously. Jeffrey tells the sitter he has to use the restroom so he can avoid inpatient hospitalization.

Is it okay for solitary closeness?

What Was That

The electric guitar case unzips as Jeffrey looks in awe. Looking around his home establishment, everything is still except the ceiling fan and burning scent from the hot oven.

One side of the case flaps open in desperation. The guitar is the body of a butterfly. The electronic guitar carrying case are the wings.

The headstock stares at him and cannot tell whether Jeffrey is an obstacle or resting point. The butterfly springs to the air and lands on Jeffrey's right shoulder.

Jeffrey takes a selfie. The butterfly looks as happy as can be. It is green. The wings flap slowly and cautiously. Jeffrey does not move because he has never witnessed anything like it before. What does it mean?

Jeffrey's friends tell him the lake house might be haunted. Jeffrey thinks of his mother who passed. Is she sitting on his right shoulder looking out for him? Is it some other spiritual being?

Lights flicker when Jeffrey's friends come over to hangout and barbeque. He thinks it is faulty wiring. A couple that sleeps in the guest bedroom hears footsteps outside the bedroom door. They hear the steps go up to the third floor. Jeffrey thinks the pair imagined the sounds.

Jeffrey and his pals continue to hang at the lake house. His other acquaintances sleep in the guest bedroom; even though they hear about the footsteps and flickering lights.

Jeffrey sleeps in a chair downstairs because it is very comfortable. Not because of the insinuations.

The neighbors hear the lake house is for sale. It is a great location. There is an incredible view of the lake in the back. All kinds of activities are available if you live there.

Is it worth all the activities if it might be haunted?

Where Is Existence

Sitting next to a person who feels wholesome, satisfaction and a sense of peace crosses the mind.

A hard cement-like tongue lies underneath the two as they find the exit in front of them.

It's dark and bushy outside the departure and very lonesome. Red, burning lights from aircrafts pass by as eyes and heads discover potential mischief.

The gated teeth lowers, and the rigid tongue maneuvers pass the fangs. Hair is blown to extreme lengths because haircuts don't exist in poisonous avenues.

Shot off the stiff surface by a wavy tongue when lethal animals become predators in life. Rose and Jeffrey fly into mid-air gravity.

Flip after flip, Jeffrey tries to yell, but the flipping force causes quietness. Mouth wide open, little mosquitoes drive their mission into Jeffrey's throat. Caught like a web spun by a spider, all the bugs collect on the inner sides of the throat. Throat is a miniature wind tunnel.

Mr. Jeffrey Andrew decides to close his mouth. It is hard for him because his whole skydiving experience crosses his mind. It is like free falling from an airplane after jumping off the wing. The high altitude causes a cold temperature to exist within the plane and on the wing. Five backflips are an amazing adrenaline junkie experience.

While skydiving tandem, Jeffrey spread his limbs to float in the sky and look at the clouds surrounding him. There is a great view of Earth's surface. Houses, streets, buildings, and the features that are attached to this planet are small.

He and his tandem instructor, who is attached to Jeffrey, does turns in the air. It is time for Jeffrey to pull the pilot chute in the parachute rig. Luckily, the two skydivers do not have to use the reserve chute in the backpack-like container.

Jeffrey grabs the left toggle to turn a sharp left in the air. The toggle is pulled so hard it feels like a rollercoaster ride. Then, the right toggle is pulled.

The tandem divers are messing around with the toggles, but they are getting close to the ground. Jeffrey pulls a little on the left toggle to turn toward their destination. After pulling on both toggles at the same time, the canopy goes down at an angle for a running landing.

After this thought, Jeffrey comes back to reality. Finally, Jeffrey and Rose escaped the venomous animal's body. It has been so long. The real world is a forgetful fantasy.

Is someone watching their bizarre existence?

Who Is Next to Me?

Riding toward Jeffrey's part-time, first day of work in his dad's car.

Wondering what he is thinking, *Is he happy Jeffrey is with him? Is full-time on his mind? Help your dad run the business with your siblings before Dad is forced to retire.*

On special occasions, Dad listens to music in the car. Most of the time, he likes peace and quiet.

Jeffrey thinks faster and clearer when there is music playing, especially when there is a person in the car.

It is so quiet. Jeffrey looks around the car at the dashboard and center console.

Jeffrey asks himself, *When did this stranger buy this car?*

www.ingramcontent.com/pod-product-compliance
Lightning Source LLC
Chambersburg PA
CBHW071317130626
46556CB00004B/1638